JAMES STEVENSON

THE WORST GOES SOUTH

GREENWILLOW BOOKS
NEW YORK

Watercolor paints and a black pen
were used for the full-color art.
The text type is Zapf International.

Printed in Hong Kong by South China
Printing Company (1988) Ltd.
First Edition
10 9 8 7 6 5 4 3 2 1

Library of Congress
Cataloging-in-Publication Data

Stevenson, James (date)
The worst goes South / by James
Stevenson.
p. cm.
Summary: Grumpy Mr. Worst, the
worst person in the world, leaves for
Florida to avoid the bother of his
town's Harvest Festival.
ISBN 0-688-13059-3 (trade).
ISBN 0-688-13060-7 (lib. bdg.)
[1. Neighborliness—Fiction.
2. Florida—Fiction.] I. Title.
PZ7.S84748Wng 1995 [E]—dc20
94-25354 CIP AC

It was a brisk October day. The worst person in the world was taking Daisy for a walk in the woods. The leaves were changing from green to yellow, brown, orange, crimson, and pink. The worst gazed at the colors.

"Absolutely hideous!" he said.

"The only good thing about autumn," said the worst, "is that you can get a bargain on apples. We'll drive over to Shipley's Orchard—it's only an hour's drive—and buy one or two."

He went to the garage and peered through the cobwebs.

"Uh-oh," said the worst.
His 1959 Edsel had four flat tires and was half buried in junk.
"I suppose I'll have to clear this out," he said.

The worst filled a wheelbarrow with the junk and
then pumped up the car's tires with a bicycle pump.

He wheeled the junk out of his garage.
He looked around.
There was nobody in sight.

He hurried across the big empty field next door. When he came to a large bush, he went behind it and dumped all the junk on the ground.

The junk made such a clatter that the worst didn't hear the police car coming up behind him.
"What do you think you're doing?" called the police officer.
"Don't shoot!" said the worst, putting his hands in the air.

"What's all this garbage, Mr. Worst?" said the police officer.
"What garbage?" said the worst.
"All around you," said the police officer.

"I—I'm cleaning up this field," said the worst.
"It's a disgrace!"
He picked up a rusty toaster and dropped it into the wheelbarrow with a clang.
"As long as you're feeling so public-spirited, Mr. Worst," said the police officer, "the town needs a favor from you."
"I'm afraid not," said the worst. "I don't do favors."

"You know there's going to be a three-day
Harvest Festival here on this field soon."
"Harvest Festival?" said the worst.
"Big tents, exhibits, livestock, arts and crafts,
hayrides, polka bands—"
"Next to my house?" said the worst, turning red.
"Three days?"
"And nights," said the police officer. "The town
wants to use your backyard for overflow parking.
Maybe two or three hundred cars, that's all.
What do you say?"
"Over my dead body!" said the worst. "That's
what I say!"

"Well, then," said the police officer. "Let's talk about illegal dumping of garbage. I can't remember—is it a $500 fine, or do they just put you in jail for six months?"

"Wait!" said the worst. "Perhaps a few cars . . . Not too many . . . "

"Thanks, Mr. Worst," said the police officer, and he drove away.

A few mornings later the worst was awakened by the sound of shouting and hammering.
He looked outside. Tents were going up everywhere.
"Stop that immediately!" he called, but nobody heard him.

Just then four farmers came up the steps, carrying a giant pumpkin.

"Mind if we leave this on your porch where it's nice and dry until the festival begins?" asked a farmer. "We'll give you a pie if we win."

"Get that thing off my porch this instant," said the worst.

The worst was having his breakfast when he heard a hideous shrieking.

"Hooo-eeee! Hoo-eee!"

A woman in overalls was standing in the backyard.
"What are you doing?" said the worst.
"Practicing," said the woman.
"For what?" said the worst.
"The hog-calling contest," said the woman.
"HOOOO-EEEE! HOO-EEE!"

The worst covered his ears.

Suddenly a herd of pigs came thundering across the yard. "I think I'm getting pretty good," said the woman.

The worst went down to the cellar and painted a sign. When it was dry, he carried it outdoors.

The sign said: PARKING $100 A DAY.

He was putting up his sign when the police officer arrived.

“Oh, no, Mr. Worst,” said the police officer. “You can’t do that.”

“How about $75?” said the worst.

“Don’t you have any community spirit, Mr. Worst?” said the police officer.

“Is that a serious question?” said the worst.

He took his sign back down to the cellar. Just then the doorbell rang.

It was Mrs. Dixon from down the block. "Will you be submitting anything to the arts and crafts show?" she said.

"Yes," said the worst. "I plan to paint a portrait."

"How nice!" said Mrs. Dixon.

"It's called 'Portrait of a Pain in the Neck,'" said the worst. "Would you care to pose for it?"

Mrs. Dixon left. The worst slammed the door.

"I've got to get out of this town," he said to Daisy. "I can't stand it another minute."

In the middle of the night the worst was awakened by polka music.
He put on his wrapper and slippers and marched over to the nearest tent. The polka band was rehearsing. When they paused, the worst stepped forward.
"Do you take requests?" said the worst.

"What would you like to hear?" said the leader.
"Total silence!" said the worst.
"I don't believe we know that one," said the leader.
The music resumed. The worst went back to bed, but he couldn't sleep.

In the morning the worst put Daisy and a suitcase into the car and drove it clanking and screeching out of the garage. He headed for the highway.

The worst stopped at a toll booth.
"How much?" he said.
"$2.50," said the toll taker.

"That's an outrage," said the worst. He handed the man a quarter. "Take this and be glad you got it." Then he drove over the bridge.

A few days later the worst was in Florida. The sun was warm, palm trees swayed in the breeze, people splashed in the surf.

"I don't know how anybody can stand this place," said the worst.

He took a road away from the ocean and into the swamps. It began to get dark.

"Better find some place to stay," said the worst.

The road turned to dirt and got bumpier.

At last he saw a light.
"This place will do," said the worst.
He got out and knocked on the door.

After a long wait a man came to the door.

"Who do you think you are, banging on my door in the middle of the night? I think I'll call the police," said the man.

"You're a motel, aren't you? Don't you rent rooms?"

"Nobody's rented a room since 1953," said the man. "I don't know why."

"Well, I want a room right now," said the worst.
"No pets," said the man, pointing at Daisy.
"She's no pet," said the worst. "She's a guard dog.
Want to see what she can do?"
"No!" said the man, closing the screen door.
"She goes through screen doors like a hot knife
through butter," said the worst.

The man handed the worst a room key. "Room 14,"
he said. "Clean it yourself. And don't be bothering
me for towels and soap and all that nonsense."
The worst started for Room 14.
"Don't dawdle," called the man. "Alligators, you know."
He chuckled.

The worst ran and unlocked the door to Room 14. The door came off one of its hinges as he opened it. A frog leaped out and a bat zoomed past.

The worst lay awake for a long time, listening for alligators.

In the morning the worst found the man sitting by the pool.

"The pool is extra!" shouted the man.

"Pool?" said the worst. "All I see is a dirty frog pond."

"And don't be whining for breakfast," said the man. "This is not some fancy spoil-you-rotten hotel."

"Oh?" said the worst. "I would never have guessed."

"You look familiar," said the man. "Ever stay here before?"

"I'm not crazy," said the worst.

"You look like me," said the man. "I wonder . . . "
"Nobody looks like you," said the worst. "Especially me."
"Are you by any chance my brother?" said the man.
"What?" said the worst. "I haven't seen my brother in forty years. He moved to"— the worst gulped—
"Florida?"
"Arvin?" said the man. "Is that you?"
"Yes, Ervin. It's me." They stared at each other for a moment.
"Well, don't expect any special rates," said Ervin, "just because you're a relative."

“I would never expect anything from you,” said the worst.
“You haven’t changed a bit.”
“Neither have you.” said Ervin. “I bet you don’t have a friend in the world, right?”
“Right,” said the worst. “And you?”
“Zero,” said Ervin. “How about some coffee? On the house.”
“No, thanks, Ervin,” said the worst. “I’d better get going.”

They were silent for a few moments. Then Ervin looked at his watch.
“Say, it’s checkout time! If you don’t get out of here, I’ll have to charge you for another day!”

The worst got his bag and put it in the car. He looked for his brother, but Ervin had disappeared. “Good-bye, Ervin,” he called.

From inside the motel came Ervin’s voice: “See you around, Arvin.”

The worst and Daisy got into the car and drove away.

When the worst got home, the festival was going on. There were crowds of people and loud music and lots of cars in the backyard. The smell of popcorn was everywhere. But the house was dark and gloomy. The worst watched the festival from his window.

In the morning the worst went over to the festival.
"Am I too late for the show?" he said to Mrs. Dixon.
"Oh, no," said Mrs. Dixon. "What is it?"
"It's a coconut with a funny face on it," said the worst.
"I did it myself."

"That's nice," said Mrs. Dixon. "Will you be coming to the polka party tonight?"
"Unlikely," said the worst. "But not out of the question."

A week later, in Florida, Ervin found a postcard in his mailbox.

On one side the postcard said:

On the other side it said:

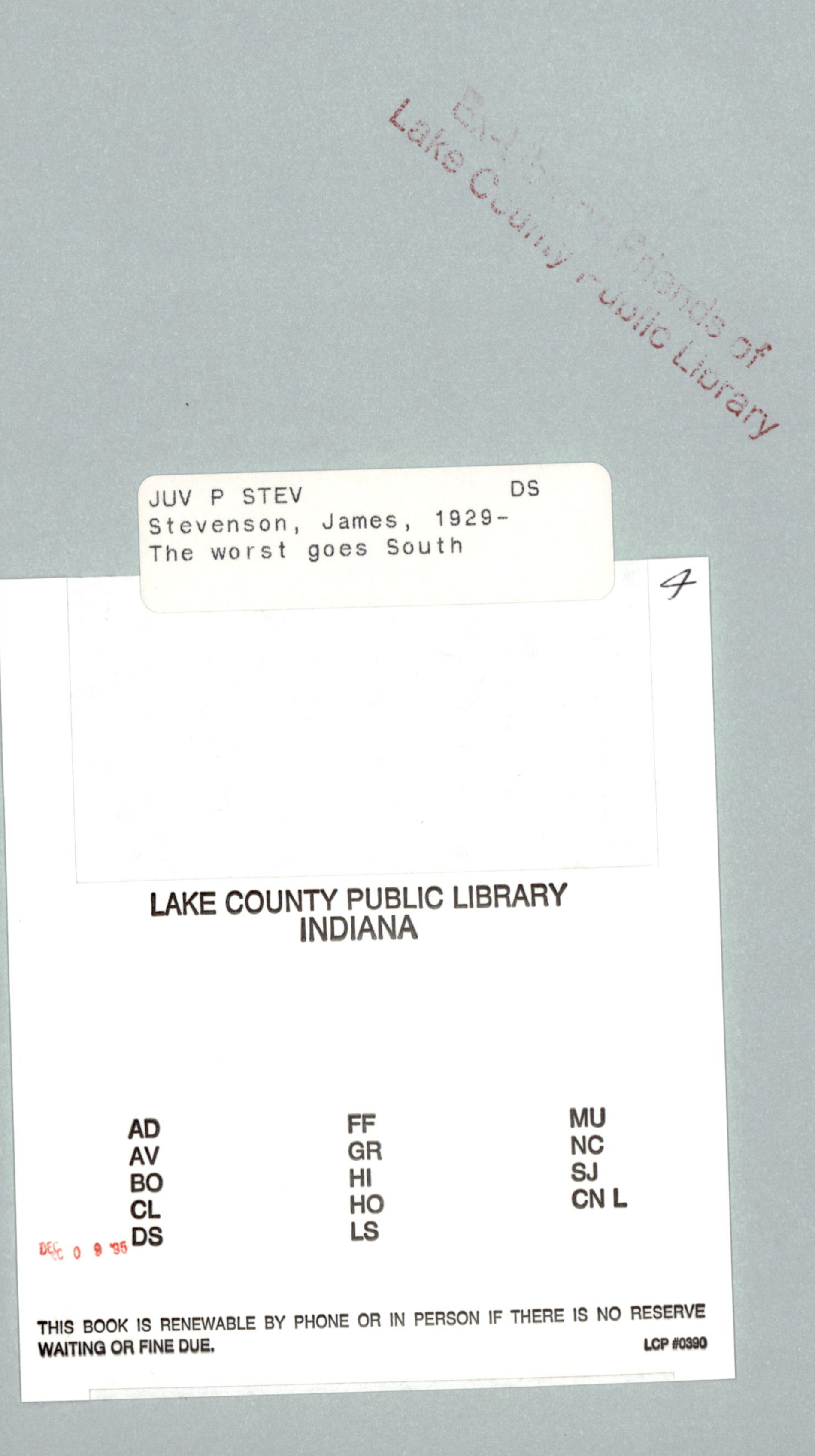